For my family, who has always supported me: my father, who introduced me to dermatology and guided my career, my mother, who introduced me to children's books and has been my best teacher, and my siblings, who have been my loyal friends. I would also like to thank Susan Youens, PhD, for her review of this manuscript.

www.mascotbooks.com

Embrace Your Skin, Embrace Yourself

For more information, please contact:
Mascot Books
620 Herndon Parkway, Suite 320
Herndon, VA 20170
info@mascotbooks.com

Library of Congress Control Number: 2021922033

CPSIA Code: PRT0222A

ISBN-13: 978-1-63755-179-0

Printed in the United States

EMBRACE Your Skin, EMBRACE Yourself

Dr. Haley D. Heibel

ILLUSTRATED BY CHIARA CIVATI

At the sound of her alarm, Gabrielle woke up on Monday morning for school.

The day started like any other, but, as she stretched and pulled her hands through her hair, she felt a clump of hair fall out. She panicked.

Gabrielle raced to the kitchen to tell her mother about her hair falling out, but her mom said not to worry. "It was likely only a few pieces of hair!" she reassured her. "It probably just happened by chance."

This made Gabrielle feel better at first, but, over the next few days, she noticed more pieces of her hair were falling out.

Am I going bald? Gabrielle thought to herself. She was scared of losing all of her hair. She admired her hair, and her friends often complimented her on it.

At school, Gabrielle tried to hide her hair loss, but, because her hair continued to fall out, people started to notice. Gabrielle's friends also seemed worried about her hair loss. Some people asked if she was okay, but others laughed at her.

After a few days of this, Gabrielle came home from school crying. She had never felt so embarrassed in her life. Inside, Gabrielle felt like the same person she had always been, but, because she had started to look differently, people had started to treat her differently, too.

Gabrielle's mom and family knew she was still the same person, though. As her mom welcomed Gabrielle home that day, she noticed her tears. She hugged Gabrielle and told her they'd find a solution.

Gabrielle's mom took her to the dermatologist, Dr. Heibel, so that they could find out why Gabrielle was losing her hair. Dr. Heibel was an expert in treating skin, hair, and nail conditions.

After examining Gabrielle, Dr. Heibel told them that her hair loss was due to a condition named **alopecia areata.** "The good news," she said, "is that your hair loss will only occur for a period of time, and your hair will likely grow back."

Hearing this, Gabrielle felt relieved to know her hair would likely come back. She smiled to herself, thinking, *I can handle that! I'm still frustrated that people are treating me differently, though.*

As Gabrielle processed the news, Dr. Heibel continued explaining and said, "Your alopecia was not caused by an infection, but by your own body targeting your hair." Gabrielle and her mother nodded, and they were relieved to have an explanation.

After her visit to the dermatologist's office, Gabrielle tried styling her hair in new ways so that it could still look pretty, even with her patches of hair loss. She found that some of the styles which showed her patches of hair loss looked even better than those that hid them!

Over the next few days, Gabrielle found that she enjoyed styling her own hair, and she became very good at it. It sparked her creativity, and she also started to knit with fabrics and began designing hats and handbags.

Meanwhile, across town another young girl named Celine could not sleep. She felt so itchy that she couldn't help but keep scratching herself. It was so uncomfortable that she tossed and turned all night! When she woke up in the morning, Celine noticed how red and dry her skin looked.

When she came downstairs for breakfast, Celine's mom and dad noticed she was having a flare, so they told her to put cream on her skin before school. Celine had dealt with **eczema,** also known as **atopic dermatitis,** since she was a baby. Both of her parents had it when they were younger, too. Celine had been having flares, or breakouts of her skin turning red and itchy, on and off throughout her life.

Celine knew that day at school would be a hard one, just like every other time she had a flare. She couldn't sit still or focus in class because her itchy skin made her so uncomfortable. It felt better when she scratched her skin, but her classmates looked at her strangely.

This is no fun, Celine thought. *Nobody wants to play with me during recess anymore, and I have to eat lunch alone.* When Celine had her flares, the other kids stayed away from her because they didn't understand why she was scratching.

One day after school, another parent even asked if Celine was scratching herself because she had bugs all over her body. Celine was too embarrassed to respond, so her mom had to explain that Celine had sensitive skin, and it wasn't from an infection or any bug bites.

Celine felt alone, even though she knew that her parents and her dermatologist, Dr. Heibel, understood her skin condition. It got even worse when she found out she was no longer invited to her friend's birthday party because her friend was worried she had a contagious skin infection.

Celine had to spend the weekend of her friend's birthday party alone just as she had spent many others. She wasn't bored, though. Instead, she entertained herself without needing friends. Celine read about so many interesting people and ideas from lands far away, and even fantasy worlds. *These characters in the stories are more interesting than all of my classmates*, she thought. Celine even had the idea to record her own talk show, where she interviewed some of the characters in her books! (They were really her parents playing pretend, but she had fun anyway.)

Two streets over, Salvatore woke up that Saturday, and, when he looked at his hands, he noticed that a spot on his right hand looked white. *That's weird,* he thought. Salvatore considered that he might have gotten something stuck on his hand, so he went to the sink to wash his hands. However, the white spot didn't go away. *Why is my hand turning white?* he thought to himself.

Over the next few weeks, Salvatore began to develop more white spots on his skin. There were some on his legs, which he tried to hide by wearing pants. However, when he started to develop white spots on his face, other kids at school started to notice.

It seemed like everyone he knew kept asking, "What's on your face?" Some kids thought he had just gotten food on his face, or had a milk mustache, but Salvatore knew they were permanent white spots.

When his classmates found out the white spots were permanent, some kids laughed at Salvatore. When he went to give high fives to the other players at soccer games, some kids wouldn't even clap his hand when they saw the white spots there. His teammates also started to leave him out at practice.

Salvatore came home from school every day feeling sad, and one evening he told his parents he was upset that he was being left out at school and soccer because of his white spots. His parents decided to take him to the dermatologist so they could find out why his skin was turning white.

After taking a look at the white spots on Salvatore's skin, Dr. Heibel explained to Salvatore and his parents that he had **vitiligo.** She educated them about his skin disease and said it was caused by his own body attacking the cells of his skin that make pigment.

"It's not caused by an infection," said Dr. Heibel. "However, it will be hard for the newly whitened spots on your skin to go back to the color they were. We will still do everything we can to get the pigment to come back with some treatments," she said to Salvatore and his family.

Over the next few weeks, Salvatore followed what Dr. Heibel told him to do. He applied the cream she gave him to the white spots, and he went to her office a few times to get a special light treatment to help the pigment come back. He was making some progress with treatment and noticed that the white spots were getting darker.

Even though Salvatore's classmates knew he wasn't contagious, they still stayed away from him and made fun of the spots on his skin. He was still being left out at soccer, too. *I wish things would get better,* he thought. *Soccer's not as fun anymore because no one passes me the ball.*

Salvatore decided that he wanted to play a new sport. He asked his parents for a tennis racket and tennis balls for his birthday, and they surprised him by signing him up for tennis lessons, too.

When the day came, Salvatore was so excited to meet his tennis coach. Coach Tony was nice to him, and he never even seemed to notice or comment on how his skin looked. After a few lessons, Salvatore realized he liked tennis even better than soccer, and he always looked forward to playing tennis with his coach.

One day, Salvatore went with his parents to the dermatologist after his tennis lesson for one of his light treatments. There were two other girls in the waiting room with their moms.

Salvatore noticed that one girl was reading an interesting book with pictures of Paris on the cover, and he asked her about it. It was Celine.

Celine noticed that one girl had a hairstyle she really liked, and she complimented her. It was Gabrielle.

Gabrielle noticed that a boy was holding a really neat green racket with special white leather stitching on the grip, and she asked him about his tennis lessons. It was Salvatore.

Soon after Salvatore, Celine, and Gabrielle met each other, they were playing in the waiting room and had the most fun they'd ever had in their lives! Salvatore, Celine, and Gabrielle were excited they had met other people who they could relate to. Their caregivers exchanged numbers so they could all set up a playdate.

The first playdate the children had was the start of a lifelong friendship. The children found out that, although they had different interests, they had similar experiences of hard times that came from having skin diseases.

"I felt sad and lonely when I was left out at soccer. That's why I started to play tennis." Salvatore shared with his friends.

"I was left out from a friend's birthday party because my friend thought my skin disease was contagious," Celine replied.

"Yes, my classmates started treating me differently when my hair started falling out. It made me feel sad and lonely, too. I don't want anyone else to ever feel like I did!" Gabrielle exclaimed.

"Neither do we!" replied Salvatore and Celine.

The children then remembered how kind Dr. Heibel had been to them and how much better they felt when she told them what their skin conditions were and helped the children treat them. She was like another mom to them! They decided to go together to the dermatologist's office with their caregivers to tell Dr. Heibel how grateful they were to have her as their doctor.

"Thank you for the difference you have made in our lives by accepting us as we are, making our skin better, and allowing us to be empowered by our experiences with our skin diseases," they told Dr. Heibel. "We would like to help other children with skin diseases so that they won't feel sad and lonely."

"Thank you," Dr. Heibel said with a smile. "That means a lot to me. This is exactly why I became a dermatologist. I think we could start an after-school program with some other children I've met like you, but we can include everyone who is interested in coming, too."

So the children started an after-school program, where more children were invited to play games, read, and play sports together. First, it began with a few other children they had met at the dermatology clinic, but then some of the other children at school who didn't have skin diseases found out about the after-school activity sessions and wanted to join in!

EMBRACE Your Skin, EMBRACE Yourself

Gabrielle inspired the other children to become more creative and make artwork. They visited the dermatology clinic one day to show Dr. Heibel their creations. "Wow, these are amazing!" she smiled. "I am excited to see that you are enjoying the after-school program. I think we could expand on our efforts and create an organization to raise money and awareness about skin diseases. We could even sell your artwork to raise money for research for treatments of these skin conditions and to provide resources for other children who cannot afford dermatologic care."

"Yes, we would love to do that!" the children exclaimed. All of the children felt motivated to help others with skin diseases after they learned what it was like for their friends in the after-school program to live with their skin conditions.

The children named the organization, "Embrace Your Skin, Embrace Yourself." They worked with Dr. Heibel to develop an event that was a huge success. The event was full of children smiling and laughing together. The paintings the children worked very hard on were sold, and the funds were used to create new treatments for skin diseases and to provide treatments for children with skin diseases who couldn't afford to pay for them.

Gabrielle, Celine, and Salvatore were overjoyed. It felt so good to help other people!

They also enjoyed working in the organization and making art and became friends with the classmates who had once made fun of them.

The difficult times Gabrielle, Celine, and Salvatore went through ended up helping them live happy, successful lives later on. Gabrielle became a famous fashion designer and hair stylist, and she even had clients request she style their hair so they would have some patches of hair loss showing. Celine became a world traveler, and she produced her own television show, filming the interesting people she met and places she saw when she traveled. Salvatore became an Olympic tennis player, and he even won a gold medal!

Gabrielle, Celine, and Salvatore learned that there was much more to who they are than how they look. The most important things were to apply their skills to serve others and to be kind to everyone. They remain friends with each other and Dr. Heibel and continue to give to and participate in their organization, "Embrace Your Skin, Embrace Yourself." They could not be happier!

ABOUT THE AUTHOR

Haley D. Heibel, MD, is a doctor pursuing a career in dermatology. Her dermatologist father inspired her passion for the field, an interest which only strengthened as she grew up and saw how skin conditions affected her peers and others. Haley is from Lincoln, Nebraska, and enjoys spending time with her family, friends, and pugs, traveling, the theatre, spending time in parks and nature, writing, and comedy.